TORTURED PANTHER'S ONE NIGHT MATE

SHIFTER DOCTOR DADDIES INSTALOVE ROMANCE SERIES

AMELIA WILSON

CHAPTER ONE

Maria

How strange it felt to no longer be on the run.

For as long as I could remember, I spent my life on the road. I traveled from town to town, seeking refuge wherever wayward shifters hid. In tunnels, in sewers, in rotten warehouses—it didn't matter.

It was where I belonged. It was where I *thrived*.

Settling on a farm under a new alpha was new to me. Though I had spent plenty of time on the Kirkland Farm, the streets were my home. Cars were my retreat from the chaos of the world around me, the never-ending pain of being lost a constant thought in the back of my mind.

That was until I met Landon.

My eyes glazed over as I stared out the community center windows, the four of them wide and clear, allowing sunlight to filter through the glass. Patches of orange sun splattered over the tiled floor where a broom appeared, connected to a little girl named Destiny.

Bright, curious eyes observed me as she paused. "You okay, Miss Maria?"

"I'm okay, dear."

"You look sad."

A sigh escaped me. Sad didn't even *begin* to cover what I was feeling. The most recent shipment—the word we used to refer to the truck that hauled survivors of tragedy to a safe place—was supposed to arrive today. I had admittedly been watching the horizon for that familiar man, the field surgeon who had stolen my attention in recent weeks.

"Landon hasn't come yet," I whispered. I cleared my throat and forced a smile, gesturing to the activity room that was still littered with books. "Let me help you clean."

Destiny hummed cheerfully as she continued sweeping.

"How's your father doing?" I asked as I gathered books from the ground, the tables, and the counters lining the windowsills. "Is he okay?"

"He's doing good," Destiny replied. "He loves my new mommy."

"I'm glad to hear that, dear."

She grinned, her two front teeth far bigger than the rest that occupied her mouth. "She's going to teach me Taekwondo!"

"That must be exciting for you."

"She says if I want to be a big and strong wolf, I have to learn how to fight."

I nodded. "That's important."

"And I want to teach the other kids, too."

"You would make a fantastic teacher."

Humming sweetly, she swept her way across the room, doing a fine job of cleaning up the dirt leftover from playground time. No matter how much we cleaned, the sand seemed to stick in all the nooks and crevices of the room, but I took pride in keeping a clean daycare center.

Sure, we only had five kids total that came in, but it was worthy of being treated with care and respect. Just like those people who were on the run.

Just like me.

I clutched my heart as though I were experiencing cardiac arrest. Something felt wrong. I couldn't quite place the emotion, my vision tunneling as I turned to the only door that led in and out of the activity room.

April barged through the cherry red door seconds later, her appearance flustered. "Maria."

I dropped the books I had gathered, the collection of them clattering loudly to the table in front of me. "It's Landon, isn't it?"

Confusion flooded her expression but was soon cleared with a look of determination. She nodded. "There's been a...complication with the most recent shipment."

"Fuck."

Destiny gasped. "Miss Maria! You said a bad word!"

I waved away her exclamation, mumbling apologies as I chased after April. Destiny was right on our heels, nervously asking question after question. We had yet to tell her exactly what Landon did. Though she had been involved at one point when we tried to smuggle her caregiver and her to safety, we still weren't comfortable divulging all of the details.

Better she was in the dark now than laying awake at night worrying about everyone.

I chased April from the miniature daycare center to her home just yards away. The three of us darted inside and gathered around Claude who was holding a phone in front of his face. That familiar masculine voice crackling through the speaker stopped my heart, causing me to freeze.

Landon is in trouble, I thought as I squinted at the phone. *He needs me.*

There was no question about it. The feeling I had gotten in the activity room was directly related to Landon. He was in trouble. No, I wasn't sure what the circumstances were, but I was about to find out—and I would do everything I could to make sure he was safe.

"...truck turned over. It's a mess, Claude."

"I'm going to get there as soon as I can."

I grabbed the phone and said, "Landon, Maria. I'm coming."

"Maria?"

"Tend to the wounded."

Claude nodded his face a picture-perfect resemblance

to a statue. He was used to being in dire situations like these. "I'll collect some shifter nurses from the hospital and then get to you. Turn on your GPS so I can find you."

"...connection...battery dying..."

I squeezed the phone tightly. "We're on the way."

I relinquished the phone back to Claude who disconnected the call. He turned to April who nodded respectfully. Destiny joined April's side, the poor little girl frightened by the anxiety clouding the air in the room.

April smiled at her stepdaughter. "Everything is going to be okay. Your daddy is going to help some people."

"Can I go?"

The three adults in the room replied in unison, "No."

Destiny cowered beneath April's arm, hiding her face in the alpha's blouse.

I smiled sympathetically as I bent forward, touching Destiny's arm so she could look at me. "You have to practice those moves so you can help next time, okay?"

"I can do that."

"Will you make sure the activity room is clean while I'm gone?"

Destiny perked up, cheered by the fact that she had a new task to do. "Yes, ma'am!"

I chuckled as I focused on April. "Would you mind?"

"Not at all," my alpha replied. "Go help your...Go help Landon. I'll be right here. Keep your phones and GPS on, okay?"

I saluted my alpha and darted outside, running all the way home.

Landon did so much for our community and the other shifter communities at large. When he was in trouble, we were all in trouble. His pain was my pain. His triumph was my victory.

After taking care of everyone else, it was up to me to do the same for him. I had to protect Landon. I had to protect the amazing field surgeon who had taken me to safety when I had no other options left.

It was all I could do to repay my debt to him.

My feet carried me without any instruction from my brain, my hand clutching at my skirts to keep them from tangling in my feet. I slid into my truck, started the engine, and peeled out of the driveway, heading danger-ously toward the exit of the farm.

A buzzing sound caught my attention. I lifted my phone from the pocket of my traditional skirt to see Claude calling me. Answering the call provided me with precise coordinates to where Landon and the crashed truck would be located.

"I'm on my way," I said into the phone before hanging up.

"I'm coming for you, my love," I said to the road ahead. "I'm coming for Daddy…"

CHAPTER TWO

Landon

Blood smeared the side of the truck, pooling in the road. The groans of pain echoing around me resembled a battlefield, reminding me of my darkest days spent overseas. Squinting against the setting sun, I scanned the area for those injured, checking limbs, eyes, faces, and head wounds as quickly as possible.

Ten people had tumbled from the back of my truck and scattered over the dirt road. If we had been discovered by patrolling shifter forces, we would have been in hot water. But the road was deserted and hadn't been used in years.

I knew because it was my typical route back to the Maxwell farm.

April had done a fine job of taking over as alpha. It was up to me to make sure the place remained a safe haven for others, whether they stuck around permanently or temporarily. That was my job.

And I took my job seriously. I took all necessary precautions to keep the people I helped safe and secure.

Failure looked awful on me. And boy, had I failed *miserably* with this accident.

The ditch must have formed recently because it caught me off-guard. I lost control of the truck, smashing into a tree that sent the truck spiraling out of control. We flipped three times.

All ten people had survived which was purely a miracle. Maybe I had some good luck in me. Or maybe it was sheer *dumb* luck that had kept us all mostly safe.

Sighing, I knelt on the ground and scooped a little boy into my arms, cradling him. The poor thing had a head wound that needed immediate medical attention. While most of the shifters had gotten away with scrapes and cuts, this one wouldn't make it if he wasn't taken to a hospital.

My eyes scanned the horizon. *Come on, Maria. Come on, Claude. Hurry.*

I turned to the woman leaning against the now battered truck. "What's your name?"

"You don't take names," she replied, wheezing as she leaned forward as she held her left side. Her russet-brown skin boasted a few cuts. "But that's Donovan in your arms."

"Donovan," I repeated to the little boy I held. He

couldn't have been more than four years old. And he reminded me of someone. "I'll get you help. I promise."

"Serena."

I focused on the woman. "What?"

"My name is Serena."

A smirk tugged my lips. "Thought you didn't want to give your name."

"Well, I changed my mind."

"You remind me of Maria."

She huffed. "That Spanish woman who follows you around like a puppy? I hope not."

"I mean, she talks like you do. Smart."

"It's my mouth that nearly got us two in trouble back where we came from.'

I nodded. "Well, you'll be safe where we're going. I'm going to see if there's much I can do for his head."

"Not with a wound like that."

Ignoring her doubtful comment—though warranted— I dove into my work, drawing on my knowledge as a field medic to patch up the wound as best I could. Our medical supplies were destroyed by the crash, but there was gauze and antiseptic cleaner to spare.

Serena held her son's head steady as his eyes rolled to the back of his head. He started shaking.

"Shit, he's going into shock," I announced. "Careful. Mind his head. That's it..."

Images of the past rushed to the surface. I thought of a little boy who must have been ten years old at this point. Dark brown eyes and umber-brown skin like mine, I was sure of it. A woman teetering on her heels, one of the spikes broken, a bottle of booze in her hand as she staggered on the sidewalk.

When I shook my head, the images disappeared. I tended to the little boy, making sure he was comfortable while I did everything I could. The sound of an approaching truck caught my attention.

Hope washed over me as the shifters around me cheered. The truck came to a stop in the middle of the road just before the ditch. They caught it before I could.

Failure, I repeated to myself. *This is all my fault.*

Maria hopped from the truck, long black hair flowing behind her as her hazel-blue eyes scanned the damage. After a quick nod, she sent a couple of shifters to help the wounded who lined the road. Claude jogged up to me, kneeling next to the boy.

"He just went into shock," I explained as I handed him over. "Head wound. It's deep, Claude."

"I'll help." He turned to Serena. "Are you the mother?"

Numb from the accident, all she could manage was a quick nod. He hoisted the boy up and nodded for her to follow.

"We're ten minutes from the hospital, but we can get there in five if we're quick about it."

The two of them disappeared into the truck as Maria lingered behind. She held her hand out to me, khaki beige skin boasting rays of the sun kissed by reddish-brown freckles as she helped me from the ground. I stood a good six inches taller than her, prompting me to tilt my head forward just so I could observe her features.

"How will we get all the shifters back without the truck?"

I shrugged. "Minimal damage to them. We can start walking."

"I'm not sure they'll like that."

"I'm sure they're used to it."

She hummed curiously, eyes turning to examine the area once more. Her critical gaze picked up on each pair of people that were being tended by shifter nurses. It *was* minimal damage.

Sheer dumb luck, I thought as I watched Maria with a look of admiration.

"You were quick."

She focused on me. "I have to be quick. You taught me that."

The smile on her face was small but playful. Her eyes lit up with amusement as she closed the gap between us, wrapping her arms around my waist and nestling her head into my chest as she so often did when things went wrong with shipments.

As soon as we were tightly locked together, the scent of a campfire met my nostrils. Sweet, dry, and earthy summer invaded my senses. Heat rushed through my limbs, overwhelming every part of me that desired her.

And she had no idea about my affection. She wasn't aware that I pined for her on every single trip I took without her by my side. No shipment was the same when she wasn't present.

At the same time, I couldn't risk her life with each trip. She had to stay behind at the farm where she could tend to the children. Our numbers were quickly growing and they would need guidance before joining one of the local shifter schools.

I nuzzled into her neck, inhaling more of her fiery scent. I could have spent all evening in her arms. But the sun was quickly setting and we had to get these people back before we lost light. I didn't have enough flashlights to go around.

"Come on," I urged, though I made no effort to move. "We should get them moving."

"We should."

Neither of us released each other. "I...guess we ought to show them the way, right?"

"I suppose that would be wise."

"Though I'm sure anyone could follow this road and find the farm."

She hummed, the sound vibrating against my chest and causing my legs to tense with a deeply forbidden need. "That sounds dangerous."

"Which means we should leave now."

"Still scouts in the area?"

I shook my head and then turned my nose to her thick hair, imbibing the milky conditioner she often used. "Not that I've seen."

"Let's keep it that way."

With strained effort, I let her go. We walked toward the collection of shifters on the side of the road, each of them sporting some kind of gauze or covering. One of them wore a splint on his right arm.

I sighed.

"Broken bones, huh?" I teased.

"Eh, I've had worse."

The kid couldn't have been older than fifteen, but he looked even younger, sprightly gaze full of hope. God, I prayed that he never lost that feeling.

I smiled warmly. "We have to walk the rest of the way. Shouldn't be more than thirty minutes."

A round of annoying groans resounded as people stood up from the ground. Maria chuckled as she looped her arm with mine. "How often do we get to have a leisurely stroll?"

"Not often."

"What a blessing."

Smiling, I observed her serene features, noticing how content she appeared with walking by my side. One quick glance back at the wreckage reminded me about the little boy, the one who had looked so similar to my son.

I have to rescue Torrance, I vowed silently as I wrapped my arm tightly around Maria. *From his reckless mother. From a reckless future.*

And I would do it even if it was the last thing that I did.

CHAPTER THREE

Maria

The medical building on the farm needed renovating but was large enough to host those who were eagerly awaiting homes of their own. Landon made his rounds to each bed, checking in with shifters who gladly gave him their names.

His eyes never left the faces of the people with whom he spoke. Each movement was calculated and carefully catered to the person in front of him. No one in the vicinity looked sour, depressed, or disappointed, especially when they got to speak to him.

I tried to imagine where he had gained such a skill. Though he rarely talked about his past, he mentioned being overseas for some time in a rather sticky situation that forced him to figure out how to heal people using just the resources he had around him. With the way he worked, he seemed to have figured it out rather quickly.

A sigh inspired me to lean my shoulder against the doorway to the sleeping area. Behind me was a series of hallways with private exam rooms, an abandoned office, and a storage room stacked with all sorts of files, papers, and documents. None of us had been brave enough to dig through it just yet.

Things were still fresh here. April was doing wonderfully as the new alpha, yet it was also more chaotic than any of us could have predicted. And with shipments coming through every month, we were in desperate need of more capable volunteers.

But Landon seemed to be able to handle it all. He entertained the adults in a way that didn't make them feel patronized. He cracked jokes. He wore his dazzling smile.

I ate it up. I couldn't help myself. Finding satisfaction in watching him work was a valued pastime. After working together for so many years, how could I not enjoy watching him work?

"Maria."

The sound of his voice was silky and smooth like an aged whiskey. Hints of smokiness lingered in his words, an alluring song that only I could hear. How much did he want me right now?

Could he tell I wanted him?

I bit my lower lip, turning my gaze to the sweet man who never raised his voice, even in emergency situations.

Careful. You know he doesn't actually want you, I warned myself. *He's just being kind.*

I smiled cautiously. "How's everyone doing?"

"Settled and comfortable for now. No serious injuries."

"Except for the child."

Hurt flashed over his eyes, gone in a split second later. "Yes, except for Donovan."

I raised my eyebrows. "You learned his name."

"Why is everyone so surprised about that?"

"I'd say it's because of your number one rule."

He held up a hand to prevent me from saying it. "No names until we reach the farm. Of course."

"You've always had that rule. Or some variation of it. How long did it take you to learn my name?"

Dark brown eyes like the bark of a tree in winter studied me carefully. The rest of his face was expression-less, but his eyes held heat, something so deeply affec-tionate that I thought I might have been hallucinating.

I blinked.

No, it was there. His irises expanded, the obvious shift revealing that his panther was floating just under the surface of our interaction. Why did his panther come forth?

"A year," he whispered. "I didn't ask for your name for a whole year."

"Even though I proved myself worthy at your side."

A smirk tugged the right corner of his mouth. "You more than proved yourself, Maria."

"I'm dedicated to making sure people are safe."

"You're the mother they need."

My brows dipped together, his words biting into me in such a loving yet painful way. He had no idea how much I wanted to become a mother—and with him. *Only* with him.

I parted my lips to speak, silenced by the way he drew close. He gently nudged me into the dark hallway where we disappeared around the corner, shadows guarding our features and our true intentions. His lips drew close to my mouth.

"I have something to do," he whispered so low that I strained to hear him over the rapid beating of my heart. "Can you mind the ward?"

"I can."

He sighed, breath dusting my lower lip and inviting me to tilt my head, preparing for impact. But I didn't make a move. I *couldn't* make a move.

I knew he would reject me.

"Maria..."

I hummed softly, the sound appearing more like a mewl than anything tame. "Yes, Landon?"

"Will you be alright here without me?"

"Yes..."

It was a bold lie. I wouldn't be alright without him, but I didn't want to reduce myself to begging. If he had something important to do, then I wouldn't get in his way.

"Can I help?" I asked as his fingers brushed against my hands. "Can I go with you?"

"No, you have to stay here."

Yes, Daddy. I didn't dare say the words out loud. It would ruin our friendship.

But god, how much I *wanted* to ruin our friendship.

"Alright," I said, stepping back from him. Just a few inches I added between us made me feel cold. "Be safe, okay?"

"I'll check in."

And with that dazzling grin illuminated by moonlight, he retreated, disappearing at the end of the hallway.

AFTER MAKING sure our new arrivals were comfortable, I went to April's house. The living room hosted a medley of blankets and pillows along with a stack of movies sitting on the coffee table. Destiny held a drawing pad on her lap with a piece of charcoal perched between her fingers.

I sat next to her as I observed the picture she was drawing. Dramatic lines depicted a figure helping people from a car wreck.

I smiled. "Is that your father?"

"Yes, he's saving the day."

"What an excellent form you have."

She grinned up at me as her mother walked into the room. April wore a tight-fitting red bodycon dress with silver heels. A smokey palette decorated her eyelids with scarlet red lipstick outlining her lips. Smiling bashfully, she shrugged. "How do I look?"

"Ravishing," I praised.

"Gorgeous," Destiny stated.

I sighed. "Is Claude able to go with you to the restaurant in town?"

She nodded. "Donovan is stable and his mother is with him, so he has about an hour or so to spare with me."

"I hope it goes well."

"Viola is just down the lane. We wanted to give her the night off," April explained as she gathered her purse. "I'm grateful you could step in."

"Well, Destiny and I were due for a movie night. Right, kiddo?"

Destiny nodded. "Maria hasn't seen the new Disney movie. We're going to watch it."

"That sounds great," April said.

She nodded to the door, inviting me to follow her to the compact foyer. Winter coats lined the hooks on the right wall with shoes piled underneath. She grabbed a light cardigan and turned to me with a small grin.

"You'll be okay?"

I shrugged. "I should be just fine."

"You're worried. I can tell."

Before I could protest, her arm joined my shoulders and tugged me into a warm embrace. Just that simple motion put me at ease. No one else could have done that except for Landon.

"I'm sure he's fine," she whispered. "He told me he was leaving the farm for a few days."

"Did he tell you where he's going?"

She sighed as she drifted from the hug, but retained contact with my arms. "No, but I trust that what he's doing is for his benefit."

"I can't ever get a read on him. Can you?"

"He's a mysterious man."

Giggling, I shook my head. "Sometimes, too mysterious."

"You like him."

"I admire him."

She grinned knowingly. "I think you do much more than that, Maria."

"I don't know what you mean."

"I'm your best friend *and* your alpha," she noted as she plucked her keys from a hook near the door. "I know how you're feeling."

I rolled my eyes, a playful smile on my lips. "Of course. How could I hide anything from you?"

"You should tell him."

"I don't think he'll appreciate it."

Her smile wavered slightly. "I think he will. You should tell him before it's too late."

Wordlessly, I gave her a kiss on each cheek and shooed her outside, locking the door behind her. I took a moment to myself to gather my thoughts.

She's right. I should tell him, I thought. *Because it's so much more than admiration. I want to start a family with him. I want us to be together...forever.*

A sigh sent me back to the living room. I had to shake all thoughts of Landon if I was going to have a good time with Destiny. I didn't want to be distracted. I wanted to have a good time.

But how could I have a good time when I had no idea where he was or if he was safe? Though I was inclined to trust his word, I couldn't stop the concern from rising. My inner wolf fought to be released so she could join his side.

Soon, I told her. *He'll be back soon. And then we'll tell him everything.*

With strained effort, I focused on the television. Destiny had already set up the movie and was nestled into the cushions next to me, her drawing pad back on her lap. Once the plot got going, I let it take me over, hoping that it would erase all the things I had been thinking so hard about—even if it was temporary.

One night's reprieve—that's all I needed. I could get back to obsessing over Landon tomorrow when the day was fresh. And then I could give the situation my full focus.

CHAPTER FOUR

Landon

Late night traffic clogged the street as I made a right on East and Third. The corner where Delia worked hosted a small group of women clad in street attire—fishnets, crop tops, and skirts so short that they would give a nun a heart attack.

I maneuvered the car to a bank parking lot that was well-lit. A few cars were scattered in the lot, likely people attending the strip of bars just across the street. I would blend well with this crowd. I looked at the part.

As soon as traffic lightened up, I crossed the road, letting my feet carry me to the familiar alleys and corners where I knew my ex-girlfriend would be. Our breakup had been explosive, a massive fight that ended with me walking out. I hadn't wanted to leave her, but it was my only option at that point.

I spent years worrying about her whereabouts and about the child I knew she kept. Part of me hoped I didn't find Torrance here, that perhaps child services had scooped him up during the time Delia had custody of him. Fighting through the court would have been pointless seeing as I was wanted by every rogue shifter organization on this side of the east coast.

Letting anyone know about my location would compromise my entire operation. I wanted to keep helping people. I wanted to make sure they were safe.

And now, it was time for me to make sure my son was safe.

Regret gripped me as I hopped onto the curb and slowly approached the four girls posing on the corner. I was sure Delia was one of them, but they were all wearing wigs, covering up their true identities. And I couldn't blame them.

The streets were rough.

A car engine popped somewhere nearby, causing my vision to blur. *No, not now,* I begged as I slowed my pace. *I have to focus. I can't leave my body.*

I fought the surfacing images, the memories of the war that made me sick to my stomach at night. As much as I did my best to cover up my reaction, part of me was aware that Maria knew my struggle. Surely she had overheard me puking my guts up in a bush whenever we were camping in the swamp during shipments.

After a few deep breaths, my vision returned, revealing a lanky woman clad in latex and fishnets standing right in front of me. Her blue eyes gleamed in the lights that flashed over the curb. Bubble gum pink hair framed her face and black lipstick decorated her lips.

She blew a bubble with her gum, popped her hip to one side, and looked me over. "Lan."

"Del."

"You need something?"

I shook my head. "Where's Torrance?"

"Safe."

"I highly doubt that. Where are you staying?"

She waved her twitching fingers, nails chipped and fraying at the edges. Night gave her a look of glory, but every set of passing headlights revealed the bags under her eyes, the pallid color of her skin, and the track marks lining her left arm.

I took her wrist gently, turning her arm to study the marks. "Still using?"

"What's it to you?" She snatched her wrist back. "Marty will be mad if he sees you not paying."

"Then, I'll pay."

I procured my wallet from my pocket, drawing the attention of the other three women. I handed Delia a hundred-dollar bill and snapped my fingers in front of her face to break her daze.

Raising her eyebrows and popping another bubble with her gum, she shrugged. "Bridge."

"Which bridge?"

"Emerson."

I sighed. "Delia, seriously? You weren't in an apartment?"

"Can't afford it."

"You can with what I gave you. At least for a week."

She hummed curiously as her eyes rolled past me, focusing on something that was fast approaching. The clap of heavy footsteps echoed. It sounded like Marty was coming up to investigate my presence.

"Ladies," I said, tipping my head to the three women huddling next to Delia. "Marty give you problems?"

"None," the one with blue hair replied.

"Nope, we're happy," the shorter one with green hair responded.

"Just fine," squeaked the tall, bulky one.

Pursing my lips and nodding, I turned around as I cracked my knuckles. Marty was a huge guy, but that didn't matter. Huge didn't really bother me. I had plenty of strength and wit to take him down with a single punch.

The guy looked mad as hell. His nostrils flared as a pink glow on his cheeks indicated his frustration. Red patches bloomed on his neck and forehead as he grew bigger with each approaching stomp. His bulky shoulders and thick torso told me he lifted plenty—and the ring on his hand speckled with blood told me he gave plenty of slaps, too.

After popping my neck to loosen my muscles, I bent my knees and curled the fingers of my right fist. Years of training prepared me for moments like this. I calculated precisely where it would hurt most on the charging man and then waited a few more seconds, letting the distance close between us.

And then, I swung.

All 225 pounds of muscle and mass flew backward, landing flat on the sidewalk with an echoing *thwack*. As soon as I saw my opening, I darted past the guy, sprinting at panther speed to avoid capture. I had plenty of practice with this as well.

The guy wouldn't be able to catch up with me. Behind, the girls on the corner cheered loudly after me, beckoning me to return. I didn't have time. I had to get to my son. Something in my heart told me that things were about to go from bad to worse.

I just hoped I could get there in time.

A LIGHT RAIN pattered against my shoulders as I approached the ominously dark bridge. Headlights swarmed the area briefly before disappearing, taking with it the idle sound of a motor. Crickets chirped loudly in the bushes as I followed a thin, winding path toward the underside of the bridge.

Two tents stood out from the darkness, their openings zipped closed. I studied the area—a fire that had once been going was now smoldering ash, empty tin cans littered the area, and a lone red hoodie with a broken zipper lay lifeless in front of the nearest tent.

Crickets continued singing behind me. A few frogs croaked, their calls reverberating against the underbelly of the bridge. The soft *swish* of my boots landing in the sand alerted me, prompting me to slow my pace and lighten my steps.

I wasn't sure if this was the right tent. If I happened to be a homeless person just trying to get some sleep, I would have to go back to Delia and try to get more information out of her. She was likely zonked out of her mind. This might not even be the right bridge.

After taking a deep breath, I tapped on the metal pole holding the tent in place. It was as good as a knock as I would be able to accomplish. Coughing erupted within the tent and then shuffled. More coughing.

The sound of the zipper struggling to move cut through the night. I took a respectful step back, hoping I was in the right place. I had to save my son from this life. He didn't deserve to live like this.

Another round of coughing. Soon, the plastic sheet dropped, revealing a haggard young boy with eyes the bark of a tree in fall. Eyes like mine. This was Torrance.

"Torry," I whispered.

The boy blinked. "Y-yeah? Did my mom send you?"

"In a way, yes."

"What do you need?"

He scooted back and shuffled toward what appeared to be a tackle box. Opening the lid revealed a medley of drugs.

I shook my head. "She didn't tell you about your father, did she?"

He coughed violently, shoulders shaking as he hovered over his knees and tried to get a hold of himself. Shit, the kid was ridiculously sick. He wouldn't last another night out here, even if it was warm outside. He needed a hospital.

"Come on, kid. We're taking you to the emergency room."

Torrance groaned. "No."

"Torry, you're sick. I'm taking you in."

"No, Mom says ER won't help."

I groaned with frustration as I hauled him from the tent and cradled him in my arms. "Don't care. I'm your father. You're coming with me."

My child should have been a healthy ten-year-old boy tucked into bed at this hour. He should have been reading a book, or watching television, or trying to quietly play a game on his console. Living in a tent under a bridge wasn't the life I imagined for him.

So, I had to make it right. I had to take him to Claude and get him the help he deserved. He was too skinny and frail in my arms, and he wouldn't last another night like this. I carried him all the way back to my car, making sure to take the darkened back alleys to avoid Marty—and Delia, too.

Knowing her, she would have a fit seeing me carrying Torrance away. It was better she was zonked out of her frickin' skull so she didn't notice me saving our son. Hell, she wasn't going to do it.

It was up to me—I had to make things right. And it all started with my son getting medical help.

CHAPTER FIVE

Maria

Not hearing from Landon all night had set me on edge.

I was able to enjoy my time with Destiny, and even appeared mostly normal by the time April had gotten back from her date, but I couldn't hide it any longer. I was upset. And I didn't know what to do.

The three shifters who were staying at the farm temporarily from the previous day's haul requested to be taken to the border of the state. Landon and I had connections that would happily meet us to transport these shifters who were on the run. And it was up to me to take them to safety.

Once everyone was loaded safely into the truck that April loaned me, I drove carefully on the predetermined route, practicing every line that Landon had taught me about dealing with both human and shifter authorities.

Getting caught with any amount of people who weren't exactly registered here was bound to cause trouble.

I wasn't about to cause trouble.

We reached the checkpoint in a matter of hours. I sighed as I hopped out of the truck, releasing the latch on the back to let the three people out into the warm dusk. Sia and Barry met me in the center of the clearing.

Sia hugged me. "So good to see you, Maria. How are you?"

"Hanging in there."

"Have you found a place to settle yet?"

A smile stole my lips. I couldn't help it. "Actually, yeah. Better than any place I've been."

Barry grinned wide. "That's good to hear. Send Landon our best, yeah?"

"Of course."

Just as I was about to turn, a figure emerged from the treeline. Barry stood guard as Sia took a friendly step forward, forever the diplomat. She smiled in greeting. "Can I help you?"

"Looking for transport," the figure replied. "Is it safe?"

"It's safe. Come on out, dear."

The figure that emerged from the trees was the last man I wanted to see on this planet. I tilted my chin up, retaining an air of elegance as I tightened my shawl around my shoulders. "Josh."

"Maria?"

Sia glanced between us. "You know each other?"

Josh laughed as he stepped fully into the light,

revealing mocha tan features, a chiseled jaw, and black eyes. The brown of his irises was so dark that it swallowed his pupils, making him appear more demonic than usual.

Tall, dark, handsome—that was how anyone would have described Josh. Yet he was far from the debonair personality that might have accompanied such features. He was a joke—a player and a loser. I didn't want to be near him.

"I need to head south," he described while holding my gaze. "Could either of you take me? I have money for—"

"Maria is heading south," Barry stated while gesturing to my truck. "I'm sure she would be happy to take you."

"I can pay."

Though I hadn't seen Josh in years, I couldn't imagine he had changed a whole lot. But the look in his eyes was on of desperation. I knew that look. It was the kind to drive a person to the edges of the world *just* to get away from whatever was causing that haunted expression.

I sighed as I waved for him to join me. "You don't have to pay. I'll take you to the neck checkpoint."

"Thank you, Maria."

He said something in Spanish to me, something I didn't quite catch—and that I didn't want to catch. No one had spoken to me like that in years with such an affectionate, heated tone.

After hopping into the cab of the truck with Josh beside me, I started the vehicle and waited for Sia to pull away first. Once I was sure the shipment was safely heading north, I turned the truck around and headed back the way I came.

The cab remained silent. That was good enough for me. Even ten minutes with Josh was simply too many. The moment we landed at the next checkpoint, I gestured for him to get out.

"You're not coming with me?" he asked.

"Why would I do that?"

He smirked. "Because you love me."

"You know I don't love you anymore. Get out."

He reached across the center console to take my hand. I slapped his cheek, knocking him toward the passenger door where his shoulder landed with a resounding *thump*. Shocked, his eyes focused on me, anger emanating from those dark circles.

"You'll pay for that," he warned. "I'll come for you, Maria."

"Haven't heard that before."

The moment his feet touched the ground, I took off, leaving him in the dust.

And that's where I hoped he would stay.

JOSH HADN'T HURT ME, but I was still thoroughly shaken by the time I made it back to the farm. I debated on whether or not to tell April about my encounter. If Josh had happened across me at that northern checkpoint, then it was very likely he could track me here to the farm.

He's not dangerous—he's just an idiot, I thought as I walked up the steps of my porch. I turned to study the farm, hoping no one noticed my expression from this distance. I probably looked a little lost.

But the feeling was so much worse than that. It was rejection, it was depression, and it was worry all mixed into one. Staring at the horizon wouldn't produce Landon's appearance. I knew that.

Still, I gripped the banister as I waited, holding my breath as night descended upon the farm. Headlights flashed over the lane. A car rattled its way toward my driveway, pulling up next to the truck I had borrowed.

Landon stepped out.

Overcome with relief, I darted into the yard and flung myself into his arms. Warmth greeted my lips as I pressed my mouth to his, a desirous mewl escaping my throat as he lifted me. I wrapped my limbs around his torso, unwilling to release him.

We kissed all the way to the front door, stumbling into the foyer when he finally set me on the ground. I slammed the door shut and yanked him into the nearest room— which happened to be the kitchen—and beckoned his mouth to return to mine.

Swept away by the way his lower lip curved into my mouth, I sighed into his touch, struggling to remove his shirt, his pants, and then his briefs. He returned the favor, ripping the shawl from my shoulders and yanking my blouse up. One of my hoop earrings got caught on the neckline of the fabric.

I chuckled as I worked the earring loose, removing the one from my left ear as well and tossing them onto the table. They clattered to the wood, echoing in the tight space. Landon resumed his task, hiking up my skirt and settling between my leg, nudging the apex of my thighs with his stiff member.

Moans rolled from my lips with each movement. Hands swarmed my body, tracing my curves from my hips to my breasts. He cupped my breasts gently, thumbs revolving my nipples and prompting them to harden. My lips parted eagerly to accept his curious tongue as he released one fervent thrust.

I mewled as my slit twitched, fluid rushing from my channel to soak my panties. He propped me onto the table, the furniture shaking unsteadily beneath my bottom as he stripped my panties away and ran the head of his member over my slit, inch by aching inch traced by the length of his staff.

My head lolled back as his lips sought my main artery. It seemed instinctive for him to locate it, teeth scraping the skin and causing me to shiver.

"What do you want?" he growled against my neck.

"Please, Daddy," I begged. "Fuck me as you've always wanted."

Grunting, he slid his shaft over my slit, parting my slit lips with an eager thrust. When the head of his cock perched at my entrance, I tensed, wrapping my arms tight around his shoulders to steady myself. Gasps overwhelmed me as my breathing labored. He was so close to being inside me, so close to joining me.

This was all that mattered. Nothing else could get in the way of our union, the tension has built between us over the past several years. How many times had I pictured this happening? Had dreamed of it?

One buck sent half his cock into my channel. I groaned with a mixture of torture and relief, digging my nails into his bare skin as he lowered his mouth to my right breast. He lapped my nipple, the already pebbled nub responding enthusiastically to his stimulating mouth. As he wrapped his lips around my nub, he sank deep, my muff swallowing him entirely.

I groaned as each stiff inch remained lodged inside me. I wrapped my legs around his torso, shivering as he attempted to retreat. I shook my head as I hugged him tightly.

"No, don't..."

He chuckled as he slurped on my nipple, curious fingers tracing my left nipple into standing attention. He smacked his lips as he surfaced. "How can I fuck you if you won't let me?"

"I want to feel this...forever..."

A growl vibrated in his throat as his gaze became resolute. "Then...I'll take it for myself."

"Daddy..."

He clapped his hand over my mouth. "I've waited too long, baby girl."

Sweeping thrusts erupted from his hips as his thighs

crowned my bottom. Smacks echoed with each pump, fluid gushing from my channel and coating his shaft. Soon, his piercing thrusts became slick, inspiring him to surge easily into me. I groaned into his palm, every moan reverberating on my lips as my eyes rolled back.

"That's it," he encouraged. "Open up for Daddy."

I parted my thighs to grant him better access, bowing forward to offer as much of my muff as possible for him to claim. So many years spent buried in desire were now blossoming into reality. How could I deny him? How could I deny *myself*?

My muff flexed around his shaft, tightening as his dedicated thrusts shifted into feverish pumps. Smack after smack sent shock waves through my body as his lips sought my left nipple, tongue circling it eagerly. Soft moans shifted into eager huffs, groans capping each of his pumps.

Warmth coiled in my gut as I lost sight of the kitchen around me. Goosebumps rippled over my skin, hot and cold waves washing over my shoulders as my brows furrowed together in desperation. Sweet relief flooded my system as he buried himself with a deep growl, teeth teasing my nipple as the base of his cock nudged repeatedly at my clit.

I shivered violently, clinging to his torso as orgasms rocked my body. His invasion proceeded, thrusts intense and eager to chase after my eruption. I knew he would blow inside me.

And I wanted nothing more.

CHAPTER SIX

Landon

Burying myself into Maria was precisely what I needed. As I pumped into her throbbing channel, I released her tit and traveled north to her neck, allowing my fangs to extend. An unearthly growl vibrated my throat as I sank my fangs into her main artery.

Drawing from her came naturally. I exploded inside her as I released her neck, blood trickling from my lips as I lapped at the wound to heal the punctures. A few more thrusts sent me spiraling as I came hard, nudging so deep that I thought I would split her in half.

She stroked the back of my neck, tracing circles into my skin as I raised my lips to hers. I kissed her lazily, drunk on the high of our love-making.

"Thank you, Daddy," she whispered. "How do you feel?"

"I feel...indestructible."

She smiled dreamily. "And you marked me."

"I did...?"

I focused on her neck, noticing the wound that now appeared to be a hickey with scar tissue. My eyes widened and I blushed as I withdrew my partially flaccid cock from her muff. I bit my lower lip as I rushed to the kitchen sink, grabbing a towel and slashing it with warm water.

"I'm sorry for the mess," I apologized as I wiped the blood from her shoulder. "I didn't mean...'

"Yes, you did mean to do it."

I met her gaze. "Maria..."

"I want to belong to you, Landon. I've wanted this for years."

"Really?"

I slid the cloth lightly between her thighs, delighting in the way her eyelids fluttered at the motion. Her hips bucked, eagerly greeting the warm cloth with undulations that made me want her all over again. Getting a hold of my desires was best. We had to clean up.

After wiping her clean, I lifted her from the table and carried her to the bathroom. I set her on the toilet as I drew her a warm bath, stroking the inside of her thigh as I waited for the water to fill the tub. Though the tub was snug, it would easily fit us both—and I wanted to bathe her.

There were plenty of gaps where I could have mentioned where I had been. I could have told her about

Torrance, about Delia, about rushing my son to the hospital because of a high fever. A million things could have been traded between us in place of the silence that had settled over the bathroom.

Yet we seemed so content to sit quietly with each other. Why would I ruin that?

A sigh escaped her as she rested in my arms. I nuzzled into her neck, tracing the delicate skin where I had made her mine. "Are you tired?"

"Very."

"Let's get you to bed."

She clutched my arm. "Please, Daddy, five more minutes."

I relaxed into the water, listening to the liquid slosh lightly against the edges of the tub. "Of course, baby girl. But then we have to get to bed."

"Okay, Daddy..."

Minutes later, I had her wrapped in a towel and resting on her bed. Her naked body called to me, every inch of skin inviting me to kiss, lick, and massage my way from her feet to her lips. She giggled as my lips grazed over her nipples.

"So eager..." she teased in a whisper. Her hand cupped my already hard cock. "I see you want more."

"And you," I whispered as I traced her wet muff. "We could go again."

"Just once more?"

I hummed. "Yes, baby girl. Just once more..."

SLEEP CAME EASILY. I woke the next morning before dawn, blue light glowing around the edges of the window curtains. I slid from Maria's arms, pulled on my clothes, and headed out before she could rouse from her sleep.

I'm forgetting something. I spun around on my heel, marched back into the house as quietly as I could, and planted a loving kiss on her forehead. I tugged the sheets around her shoulders and smoothed her hair from her face, watching her eyelids flutter in her sleep as a smile cracked over her lips. *That's better.*

Heading to the hospital this time was much quicker. When I had Torrance in the back, it felt like I had hit every damn red light in the county. But I got him to Claude. And Claude got him hooked up to a saline drip immediately.

Today, I hoped to find that my son was well on his way to recovering. Though I was prepared for the worst— as always—I tried to retain my hope. He *had* to be okay. I had to prove to him that I was a good father.

I wanted to be worthy of his love just as I wanted to be worthy of Maria's love. Since claiming her, my strength had doubled, my stance much more confident and my muscles thicker than they had been just hours before we hooked up. She was the key to me becoming the father I knew I was deep down.

And Torrance would complete us as a family.

I can't forget Delia, I considered as I maneuvered

through the maze of sterile hallways to Torrance's room. *She needs help. She deserves to have help.*

I paused in the doorway of my son's room. Claude stood at the end of the bed with a clipboard in his hands, brows furrowed together. I knocked lightly on the door, drawing his attention.

Recognition filled his features as he turned to me. "Landon, good morning."

"Good morning. How is he doing?"

"He's stable."

I nodded. "And...?"

Claude smiled warmly. "And he's responding well to treatment. The infection was bad, but with a round of antibiotics going and plenty of salines, he'll be back in no time."

I sighed with relief, my shoulders deflating as though I had been holding up a great weight. In a lot of ways, I had. Carrying Torrance through dangerous backstreets and avoiding his mother just to get him here had been a task. It took all my strength to drive carefully and quickly.

Another sigh sent me across the room to Claude. I tugged him into a brotherly embrace, locking my arms tight around his massive torso. He was much bigger than me, practically a tank, but his looks were surprisingly opposite to how he truly was inside. To us, he was a teddy bear.

Realizing I needed the comfort, he embraced me, giving me a quick squeeze before releasing me to my son's company. Torrance wasn't awake, but I could tell that he was dreaming. I sank into the bed next to him, resting my hand on his cheek.

"He's so small," I noted. "Why is he so small?"

"Your son is highly underfed, Landon. Where did you find him again?"

I sighed. "Under a damn bridge."

"Alone?"

I nodded.

"I can get him in touch with a nutritionist who will help get him back up to par with his peers. Physical therapy would be helpful as well seeing as his muscles have atrophied."

"Fuck." Tears flooded my vision, burning my retinas. "That dumb *bitch*."

"I assume that would be his mother."

I turned my angry tears away from my son, not willing to allow him to see me this way if he happened to wake. I swept them away, the rage remaining as my tears dried up. "Delia is an addict. She doesn't know any better."

"I can get her help, too. You just have to bring her to me."

"That'll be a task in itself."

He hummed. "We have...special rooms for shifters who aren't too keen on being treated."

"I thought you needed consent?"

"They *do* give us consent. It's later when they decide to change their mind during detox."

I sighed heavily. "I don't think she'll agree at all."

"It's a very simple program. Depending on her habits,

we can have her detoxed properly and stabilized in about six weeks or less."

"I'd like that. I want that for my boy," I said as I studied my son. His eyelids fluttered. It looked like he was about to wake up. "Torrance?"

My son hummed curiously as he raised his fists to his eyes. I caught his wrists to keep him from rubbing the crust around the corners of his eyelids. That was the infection.

I took a warm rag from a bowl next to the bed and gently wiped his eyes clear. When I was done, I held his hand, smiling when he squeezed my wrist.

"Dad," he said with a clear voice. "Where's Mom?"

"She's still..." I choked back the words. I didn't really know where Delia was, did I? Lying would be shitty. "I don't know, kid."

"On the street."

"Likely."

He nodded slowly. "There's a man who's been pushing her around and making her do things. I haven't been able to help her."

"Marty?"

Another nod. "I don't know how to help her."

"I'll help her, okay?"

"You promise?"

I nodded firmly, squeezing his hand in mine. "I promise, Torrance. I'm not leaving again."

"Why did you leave the first time?"

Suddenly, he looked like that sweet little toddler who

I had left with his mother when she wouldn't let me help her. Tears returned, causing my jaw to ache as I clenched my teeth together.

"Because of your mother," I replied. "But I'm going to help. I swear."

My son sagged into the mattress, exhaustion taking him over. His eyelids drooped as his grip on my hand relaxed. He was falling back to sleep. Good—he needed it.

I turned to Claude who had witnessed our entire conversation. "You won't tell anyone?"

"Not a soul. Not even April. Not until you say so."

"Thank you."

He hummed. "I do my best."

"You're a good friend, Claude," I praised. "I'm glad to know you and I'm proud to call you my brother in our pack."

A commotion exploded down the hallway, shouts and scuffling echoing their way to the room we occupied. Claude cocked an eyebrow and headed out to investigate. Grunting and another round of scuffling followed his disappearance.

I stood like a statue next to Torrance, making sure I could protect him. No one was getting into this room, not if I could help it. I marched to the door and locked arms immediately with a familiar figure—Marty.

And by the way, he grappled with me, I wasn't sure I could take him this time.

CHAPTER SEVEN

Maria

Rays of sun kissed my cheek, pulling me softly from my world of dreams where Landon and I had a huge family on our very own patch of land. I smiled as I reached for the body next to me, hoping to go another round before I had to get to my responsibilities of the day.

But all I found were cold sheets.

A gasp inspired me to sit upright. I clutched the sheets to my chest, searching with blurry vision for the figure I knew should have been there. Landon—he had spent the night. Was he making breakfast?

I sniffed the air. Nothing. I slid from the bed and tugged a robe around my body, inspecting the bedroom. I didn't see his boots, or his pants, or his underwear.

Peeking around the corner of the bedroom doorway revealed that Landon wasn't in the living room either. He wasn't in the bathroom or the kitchen. He wasn't in the foyer. Glancing out the window showed me that his car was gone, too.

I let the curtain fall back into place, darkness splashing across my vision.

I should have known, I reflected tearfully as I went to the bathroom. I flipped on the light, dropped the robe, and turned on the shower, extra hot. *I'm just good for a quick fuck. I don't get to live happily ever after.*

Since he marked me, I figured he would stick around. I thought he was committing to me in the way I had always wanted, becoming the Daddy to me that I knew him to be. All of his time was spent taking care of others. I wanted to give that back to him.

But I guess he didn't want me.

Sniffling, I stepped into the hot stream of water, groaning as the heat infected my stiff and sore muscles. We had gone several rounds after our initial hook-up. Feeling the soreness from him pounding me should have brought happiness, but it only brought disappointment and betrayal.

Daddy had abandoned me. What was I going to do now?

I'm going to do what I always do, I told myself. *I'm going to take care of those kids and pretend like nothing is wrong.*

I squeezed my eyes shut. Maybe running into Josh had been a sign from the universe. Taking that offer would have been significantly better than having to wake to an empty bed. It was so cold in here despite the hot water pelting my skin.

More heat—that would fix everything.

I adjusted the temperature of the shower, hissing at the boiling hot water that pricked my skin. I bore the pain, closing my eyes and dunking my head repeatedly to wash away Landon's scent. Fall leaves, moist earth, fresh petrichor—all of that belonged to him.

And he didn't belong to me.

Carrying his scent with me through the day would be an embarrassment. But what was worse was the mark that now sat fixed on my neck. Everyone would see it. Everyone would know.

A shifter who bore the mark of a potential mate without having been claimed properly always ended up withering away within a month. The heartbreak alone was enough to take down a fully grown lion shifter, even a strong wolf shifter like me. I had to prepare for the dark days ahead.

There were so many I had to face.

After my shower, I wrapped myself in the fluffy robe and stood in front of the mirror, studying my appearance. Something was different about me—something was brighter despite the fact that I had been abandoned. How did I look like this when Landon hadn't stuck around?

My fingers fell instinctively to the mark that Landon had left on my neck. *Why would he claim me if he was just going to leave me behind?*

Touching the mark prompted the same reaction I had

when Landon touched me. I closed my eyes for a moment, gently caressing the sensitive tissue as I inhaled the scent of fall leaves and dry earth. He was nearby. I could sense him.

When I opened my eyes, I shook myself out of my strange trance. No use getting hung up on the fact that Landon had taken off. Maybe it wasn't so bad. Maybe it was better this way.

Forlorn and dejected, I wandered back to my bedroom to get dressed. I had to head over to the community center for my usual morning tasks. Destiny would soon be on my doorstep, all dressed up and ready to get to work. She was a reliable and constant orb in my life.

Unlike Landon.

I sighed as I pulled a white blouse over my head and then tucked the blouse into a black skirt. I wrapped a red sash around my waist and inspected my appearance, noticing the darkened areas of fabric that hosted drops of water from my hair.

A quick blow dry produced my usual look: bangs curled over my forehead with long strands of black hair decorating my shoulders. I wrapped a red shawl around my neck to cover the mark. Just as predicted, Destiny was waiting for me on the porch. She took my hand in hers and smiled up at me.

"Don't be sad," she whispered. "He'll be back."

I blinked. "How did you know...?"

"Mom says I'm special."

"You sure are."

She beamed as we walked leisurely toward the community center. She didn't say another word, but I was tempted to press her for details. What did she know about Landon and me? What had April mentioned?

Opening the center was easier said than done. The hinges on the door desperately needed to be replaced and the locks were rusted. I made a mental note to let April know about it as soon as Destiny and I walked into the activity room. It was as clean as the day before.

I sighed as I planted my hands on my hips. "You ready?"

"Yep, I'll set up breakfast."

I smiled. "Good girl."

The day went by without much incident. The usual round of children came through, four in total, ranging from toddler to preteen. Though there wasn't a ton to do around the community center, we made do with what we had, and there were always empty fields where we could roam and play.

As I gathered the kids to bring them back to the center, April jogged after us, panting by the time she reached me. She planted a hand on my shoulder and whispered, "Hey, I have news."

"What?"

"Claude just called me."

I gripped her hand, my heart hammering as my mark burned viciously. Why was it doing that? "Landon?"

"Yeah, let's get the kids inside."

Destiny, picking up the gravity of the situation,

corralled the four children and herded them toward the back door of the community center. Once we were all safely inside, she grabbed a book and sat in the middle of the rug, inviting the kids to sit around her.

"What a perceptive child," I whispered to April as we wandered to a corner for privacy. "It's like she already knew..."

"She's special."

I chuckled. "So she told me."

"She has a sort of...sixth sense or something with shifters."

"She comforted me this morning. I didn't even know why."

April nodded. "Well, that's probably because she could feel what happened."

My expression withered, concern etching into my features. "What happened to Landon?"

"He's in rough shape at the hospital." She gripped my shoulders to keep me from falling over. "But he's safe, Maria. Don't worry."

"Oh, I'm worried. I thought he left me. I thought..."

She shook her head. "I'll let him explain, but Claude says he needs the night to rest."

"Can you tell me anything else?"

"He got into a fight."

I frowned. "With?"

"Claude said a guy came charging into the hospital. Landon helped handle the situation."

A proud smile crossed my lips. That was my Landon

—always at the forefront of any situation to get it under control. I was willing to bet that Claude and him made a great team.

April mirrored my smile, nodding. "He had gone in early this morning to help Claude."

"Wow, I feel like such a fool."

"Why?"

I shook my head, peeked over her shoulder to make sure the kids were occupied, and then pulled part of my shawl down to reveal the mark.

April's eyes widened. "Oh my god, Maria!"

"Shh!"

She giggled as she covered her mouth, reaching tentatively out to trace the mark. "You're his."

"Apparently."

"That's why Destiny comforted you. I bet you felt what he felt."

I shrugged. "Sort of."

"Mine gets like that, too, with Claude. I can always tell when he's in distress."

"He didn't tell me where he was going. He left this morning without saying anything."

April made a face that was a mixture of disbelief and annoyance, her eyes rolling to the ceiling and then settling on me. "Okay, that's stupid."

"Right?"

"Claude does that sometimes, too."

I shook my head. "What in the world are we going to do with those boys?"

"Well, right now, all we can do is let them do their thing."

She squeezed my shoulders gently and then let her hands trail to my hands. As soon as she squeezed my fingers, relief swept through my body. Warm, soothing waves washed over my shoulders and I closed my eyes, focusing on the love my alpha was showing me.

"Thank you, April," I whispered as I opened my eyes. "I needed that."

"I could tell. Do you want to talk about anything?"

I shook my head. "I should get back to the kids."

"I can stay with you and help. Would that be alright?"

"No serious alpha duties today?"

She grinned as she tugged me back to the children. "That can wait."

I knew better than to argue with April when she had her mind set on something. If she insisted on staying with me in the community center, then I would be glad to have her company. It made the day much easier to handle.

By the time all the children were picked up, Destiny and April had cleaned up the room. Everything was done sooner than usual and I smiled as I walked with my best friend and her daughter out to the lawn.

"Come over for dinner," April offered while wrapping an arm around Destiny's shoulders. "It'll keep your mind off things."

"Yeah, that's..." I trailed off, glancing at my home that wasn't more than a stone's throw away. "That's probably for the best."

"You worry too much."

I rolled my eyes. "And you don't?"

"You've been worrying about Landon for years. I can tell."

"Don't start this again."

Destiny perked up. "Start what again?"

"Nothing," April and I responded in unison.

The two of us shared a giggle as Destiny stared at us. Back at her house, I sank into the couch and tightened the shawl around my neck. That was something Destiny didn't understand yet and I didn't want her stepmother to have to go through an awkward explanation without her father present.

I tried to help April with dinner, but she shooed me from the kitchen, insisting that I needed a break. I sat with Destiny, watching the girl's talented fingers draw a gorgeous charcoal portrait of Landon and me standing in the fields. As I placed my hand over my heart, I smiled warmly, knowing that the abandonment I felt this morning was completely gone.

What a roller coaster, I thought. *Next time, I won't jump to conclusions so easily.*

CHAPTER EIGHT

Landon

The sun had yet to rise—and I had yet to sleep. Various scents lingered in the air, all of them reminding me that I was in the hospital. My right eye had swelled up and my left rib was cracked, but ultimately, I was fine.

I just needed to rest.

Delia is still in danger, I considered as I went over the events of yesterday morning. *If I hadn't injured myself in that fight with Marty, I could have gone to get her. I could have saved her.*

No amount of regret in the world could have prevented what had occurred. Marty was hellbent on locating Torrance and me, and he was dedicated to making sure we paid for whatever transgressions he thought we had committed. I shook my head, my neck aching from the motion, but I did it regardless of how painful it was to do.

That jerk had cost my precious time. Right now, Delia could be strung out somewhere on the street. She could be under that awful bridge struggling with an illness of her own. If Torrance had gotten sick, then she had likely gotten sick, too.

Even something as simple as a cold could take her out. And I didn't want Torrance growing up without his mother around. No, she wasn't exactly fit to parent him, but she could still see him while she got help.

Claude had offered special doctors and treatment. As tempting as it was to keep her around here, the idea was selfish and dangerous. Sending her to Florida, to the treatment center down there specifically designed for shifters, would be a lot better. Removing her from her usual haunts would do wonders.

But what did I know? I never settled anywhere until April invited me to live on the farm. I had spent my entire life on the run, transporting people to safety and ignoring my desire for a family.

I had already messed up one family. Why would I dare destroy another?

I tightened my fingers on the bed sheet, balling it up in my fist out of pure frustration. Injuring myself did no one any favors. And sitting here beating myself up internally wouldn't help either. I had to get myself together and come up with an actual plan.

After a few deep breaths, I glanced at the doorway,

noticing the light that spilled from the hospital hallway and cut a rectangular shape into the tile. A figure blocked part of the light and cast a shadow in the shape, prompting me to glance up.

"Torrance?"

My son shuffled with a turtle-like slowness into the room as he held the transportable IV hanger. The wheels squeaked as he slid it into the room and followed after it. He shuffled to my bed and collapsed on the edge of the mattress, exhaling loudly.

With strained effort, he gave me a smile. "Hi, Dad."

"We never got to formally meet, did we?"

"Not exactly."

I nodded and pursed my lips thoughtfully, wondering what he thought of me. I didn't dare ask. "How do you feel?"

"Better."

"You look better. How's your fever?"

His smile widened, less strained this time. "Gone."

"Claude is the best doctor around."

"The best *shifter* doctor."

I chortled. "So, you know about your roots."

"I started shifting early. Mom said you did when you were a kid, too."

"Your mother..." I let the words fall from my lips, feeling the weight of them. "I'm sorry."

"She's in trouble, Dad. She needs help."

I nodded. "I know. I have a plan."

"What's your plan?"

"You know, you talk like an adult. You're barely ten."

He chuckled. "I'm eleven."

"Oh, I guess I didn't realize…"

"I just had my birthday last week."

Tears sprang to my eyes. I had missed so many birthdays, so many warm and loving times with my son. As a tear escaped my eye, he took my hand and squeezed it.

"I'm so sorry, kid," I whispered shakily. "I didn't mean to be gone this long."

"Claude told me how you rescued people."

I nodded slowly, unable to speak.

"He said people trust you. He said that you get things done."

"That's true."

He exhaled slowly. "So, I trust you."

"Already?"

"You helped me. And you look like you want to keep helping me."

A radiant smile stole my lips. "I'll keep trying."

"So, how are we going to help Mom?"

I told him about the facility down in Florida. When I recovered from my injuries, which wouldn't be very long, we could grab her from the street, feed her, and then take her here to start some of her detoxing. After that, we could take her to Florida.

A knock interrupted our conversation. I glanced up to see Maria standing there with a teddy bear in her hands, a look of confusion on her face as she stepped tentatively into the room. She regarded Torrance with a curious expression that shifted to concern when she looked at me.

"Lan..."

I hiccuped. "Hey, I..." I shook my head. "I should have told you..."

"You damn right, you should have."

"Maria, language."

Torrance laughed. The sudden bark of amusement cut through the hushed energy of the room, inspiring Maria and I to chuckle nervously.

"Dad, I've heard so much worse," he told me. "Who's this? Is that teddy bear for me? I'm too old for that, you know."

"Oh, this?" Maria held up the bear. "It was for...Well, Landon."

"Me?" I chimed in while beckoning her to the bed. "I promise I look worse than I feel."

"Claude said you got into a fight."

I nodded. "It's...a long story. Maria, I have someone I want you to meet."

I took her hand as soon as she was next to me and then took my son's hand. I glanced between them, my heart pounding wildly as I realized what was happening.

My past and my future were joining together. And I wasn't sure how it was going to go.

"Maria," I whispered shakily. "This is my son, Torrance. He just turned eleven."

"Your son?" she repeated, shock bleeding from her eyes. "You have a *son*?"

Trying to retain my smile, I nodded. "Yeah. He was sick. I had to rescue him. He was with his mother and..."

"And now I'm better," Torrance finished for me. "It's nice to meet you, Maria."

She extended the bear as though unsure of what else to do. Beaming, Torrance accepted the bear despite what he had just said about being too old for it. He cuddled it into his lap and reached for her hand, turning her delicate fingers over and back again.

This was it. This was the most important moment of my life. Marking Maria had been a significant event, but this was so much greater than that, so much more intense. I watched with bated breath as the two of them stared at each other for a long time.

Torrance never lost his smile. It seemed to transfer to Maria, her features smoothing into an expression of serenity as she clasped his hand in hers. Then, she drew him into a warm hug, one that emanated unconditional love and protection.

Releasing him with a shaky sigh, she turned to me, tears trickling from her eyes. "You never told me..."

"I was afraid you would think less of me."

"How could I ever think less of you?"

I smiled weakly. "I underestimated you. That will never happen again, my love."

"I like the sound of that."

"And I think that's my cue to leave," Torrance announced as he stood up. He gave Maria another hug and said, "Thank you for taking care of my father."

"Of course," she replied.

I watched as my son shuffled out the door and to the right, returning to his room. Claude would soon be in to check on him, I was sure. Until that time, I had some catching up to do. I motioned for Maria to close the door.

After the door was shut and locked, she darted to the bed, dropping into the mattress next to me and slamming her lips into mine. Huffing desperately, I returned her affectionate kisses with eager lips, unable to contain my desire. Her hands swept over my torso lightly and cupped my quickly hardening cock.

I gasped as I bucked into her hand. "Not now, baby girl."

"But I missed you."

"We have plenty of time for this later."

Her fingers continued to massage my shaft, inspiring the tip of my cock to weep fluid. I shuddered as I clutched her shoulders, urging her to remove the shawl that sat in the way. I wanted to see what was mine. I wanted to see the mark.

Pink tissue raised in the shape of a mouth appeared and I smiled, extending my tongue to trace the wound. She cooed softly as my tongue trailed south, traveling over the edge of her blouse. Without hesitation, she tugged the fabric down, revealing her plump breasts for me to devour.

I lapped and sucked at her nipples as she slid her curious fingers beneath the sheet to my rigid cock. Steady strokes enveloped my shaft, her velvet skin comfortably warm against my staff.

"I just want to please you, Daddy," she whimpered. "Let me please you."

"You're such a good girl," I praised as I hiked up her skirt. I found her muff easily, the warm folds of her slit welcoming my eager fingers. "You already please me."

Strained mewls echoed from her lips as I sucked her left nipple into my mouth. The nub hardened easily under my dedicated sucks as I stroked her muff lips, drawing long, contented sighs from her mouth. Her strokes steadily increased, becoming fervent pumps that urged my hips to respond.

In a few short minutes, I blasted into her hand as she shuddered and throbbed around my fingers. I raised my hand to my mouth and sucked her nectar from my fingers, enjoying the sweet taste of her fluid on my tongue. I glanced drunkenly up at her as she continued stroking my shaft, my cock still hard from her talented hand.

"Tell me the plan," she whispered. "So I can help you, Daddy."

Already, my cock was throbbing for more. I alerted her of what needed to happen as she palmed the head of my cock, squeezing and stroking intermittently. As much as I wanted to bury my cock deep inside her channel, we had things to do.

Words fell to the wayside as I nudged into her breasts again. I could have stayed here all day. Nothing else existed when her curves were pressed to my body, her plump breasts occupying my mouth in every way. And I never wanted it to end.

Another plan surfaced, one that reminded me of the fact that she belonged to me—and I would make sure that I cemented that fact for the rest of our lives.

CHAPTER NINE

Maria

An hour after I arrived at the hospital, I curled up on the mattress with Landon, spent from having stroked him into shivering fits three times. I didn't need to get off, not when Daddy needed so much attention. I wanted to make sure he knew I would do anything for him.

Our cuddle session didn't last particularly long—at least, not for me. Claude knocked on the door and I went to unlock it, blushing as I stepped aside to allow him entry. Torrance was right behind him.

With sunlight spilling into the room, it felt less like a hospital and more like a place where a family could gather. The rising warmth in my chest alerted me that this *was* my family now. Claude, Torrance, and especially Landon had become part of my life in a way that couldn't be denied. And I would spend the rest of my life making sure they felt as I did right at this moment.

"What's the plan?" Claude inquired in a low voice. He peeked over his shoulder, nodding for me to close the door. When he turned back to Landon, he whispered, "I have a room ready for her, but how will you get her here?"

"We have to go at night," Landon replied while sitting up. He gasped as he clutched his left side.

I flew to the bed immediately, urging him to return to his horizontal position. "Honey, you can't possibly move in this condition."

"I have to be the one to convince her."

Torrance sighed as he stepped forward. "Dad, I can do it."

"No, son. It's too dangerous for you to—"

I patted his shoulder gently. "I'll go with him."

Landon blinked, shock registering in his features. "You can't."

"I can," I said firmly while holding his gaze. "And I will."

"Maria, those streets are full of sick people."

Torrance cleared his throat, squaring his shoulders as he focused on his father. "And I know them better than anyone. Mom will respond better to me, anyway."

"I think he's got a point, Lan," I stated confidently. "She'll respond best to her son. She'll resist your efforts because she doesn't want help."

"And if she ignores me, well..." Torrance scrubbed a

hand over his tight, black curls. "Well, we'll get there, right?"

"Kid, you're too young for this," Landon said weakly. He coughed, cringing as he held his left side again. "But I'm proud that you're strong."

"I'll get her. Don't worry, Pop."

Landon smiled crookedly, reaching for both of us. The pressure of his grip was a comfort. I knew better than to oppose my Daddy, but sometimes, I had to be the one to protect him. It was my turn to prove that I could be useful.

His entire life had been dedicated to others. Now, we could show him how much he meant to us while also making sure we honored his desires. This was important to me because it was important to him. After a family moment, I took Torrance with me into the hallway and smiled.

"We should eat first, okay?"

He nodded, a forlorn look in his eye. Even though I didn't know him very well, I could tell that he was worried about his family. They meant so much to him. Without hesitation, I wrapped my arm around his shoulders and hugged him to my side.

Weak hands wrapped around my torso as I led him back to his room. We ate a quick breakfast and Claude examined the child, making sure his fever and symptoms were completely gone. The fact that he had made such a quick recovery was surprising, but to be anticipated with such young shifters.

Going over the plan once more put me at ease. We had a long night ahead of us—and we had a lot to prove.

RESTING provided Torrance and I plenty of energy to handle our task. I drove us into the part of town where Delia would be working and parked where Torrance instructed. I followed his lead, knowing that he had knowledge of these streets that I couldn't have possibly picked up just from walking around. I probably would have gotten hurt.

A few sharp turns later, we were standing at the mouth of an alleyway, staring at a busy intersection occupied by four scantily-clad women. The one with pink hair swayed dizzily. Torrance shuddered and took my hand.

"That's her," he whispered. "Wait here."

I squeezed his hand, frantically trying to keep him close. Though he wasn't my child, I felt responsible for him. Not only had I brought him out here without any backup, but I had been entrusted by his father to keep him safe.

But it was more than that. I harbored an innate urge to keep him close to my body. A motherly instinct had surfaced with him, one I only felt when I was transporting others to safety. With him, the feeling was much stronger, my wolf bristling under the surface of my skin and watching for danger.

My eyes followed his every move. He tapped his

mother's arm and held her attention, drawing her slowly toward the opening of the alley where I stood. When he was within hearing range, I listened intently to what he was saying to her.

"Whatever you choose is up to you," he told his mother. "But I want to get you help. Dad wants to get you help. We have a safe place to go."

Emotions warred on her face. It was hard to get a clear view of what she was thinking. I never met her in my life, yet I felt so strongly for her, so protective of her independence. This life was killing her slowly—and I think she knew that.

Delia reached for her son, stroking his cheek gently. He gave her a warm smile, one that reassured her that everything would be okay. If it were me, I wouldn't be able to say no. That sweet, innocent smile was everything.

"To Florida, huh?" she teased as she wrapped him in a tight hug. "I guess that keeps me away from Marty."

"Come on, Mom. I have a way out."

"You sure are brave."

I smiled as they approached. Delia paused just on the other side of the shadow guarding the alley, sniffing the air when she caught a whiff of me. She clutched Torrance to her who begged her to calm down, and then he explained who I was.

Hesitantly, she took my hand, still sniffing the air curiously. I let her catch hold of my scent. Surely after so many years on the street, this was her way of becoming familiar with those around her. I let her do her thing, smiling the whole time. At least she wasn't yelling at me as Landon had warned.

"You smell like...Lan," she whispered. "God, is he okay?"

"He's just fine, Delia," I replied. "I'm Maria. I'm his mate."

"Mate," she repeated as though she couldn't believe it. "My God, how long has it been?"

Torrance tugged on her forearm. "Too long. We have to go now before Marty notices you're gone."

Another glance at the street revealed that we were safe for the time being. I led Torrance and Delia back to the car, taking a few extra turns in case Marty picked up on our scent. As soon as we were safely in the vehicle, I drove Delia to the hospital where Claude accepted her into his care.

Delia clutched me tightly. I gasped when she embraced me, stunned and moved all the same by the motion. As I returned her embrace, Torrance joined us.

And then, she was gone.

I walked Torrance to his father's room where Landon was sleeping peacefully in bed. It brought me to hope to see him resting, to see that his bruises and wounds were healing up nicely. Soon, he would be back to his former glory.

Even better than that, he would be stronger. *We* would be stronger.

I rested my hand over him as I watched his chest rise and fall rhythmically. Torrance took the opposite side of the bed, leaning close to study his father's features. He drifted back and looked at me, curiosity in his gaze.

"Where will we go?"

I smiled. "To a nearby farm where the alpha will welcome us. You're my family now. I'm going to help take care of you."

"So...you'll be like a mom to me?"

"If you would let me, yes. I would love to be a mother to you, Torrance."

He grinned weakly. "I think I would like that, Maria."

"Me, too..."

CHAPTER TEN

Landon

A week after leaving the hospital, Maria and I took Torrance with us back to the farm. We introduced him to April, Destiny, and a handful of the other kids as well as April's dedicated assistant, Dante.

Delia had been safely transferred to a facility in Florida, one that I had personally checked before admitting her there. The trip had exhausted us, but we had taken it as a family, the three of us unwilling to part with each other after so much chaos.

Destiny grabbed Torrance's hand and grinned at me expectantly. "Can Torry and I shift in the forest?"

I glanced at April. "What do you think?"

"I think these kids deserve a day of playing," April agreed. "Viola and I can watch them. You and Maria should settle in."

"Thank you, alpha."

She grinned widely as she gestured behind her, taking a collection of kids toward the treeline. Viola caught up with them easily, laughing when one of the overeager toddlers began stripping immediately, leaving a trail of clothes behind him.

I reached into my pocket, tracing the curve of the gold band that sat inside. As tempting as it was to shock Maria right now, I didn't want to put any more pressure on her publicly. I wanted her to think critically about our relationship and to make an informed decision for herself.

But first...

"Let's settle in," I suggested as I led her back to her home—*our* home. "I have something for you."

"Please, tell me it's in your pants," she whispered back in a sultry tone.

I froze for a second but urged my muscles to keep moving as I realized she meant something else, something far sexier than a ring. I smirked as we walked into the foyer and crashed together, our lips seeking each other with heated groans.

One week without her body tangled in mine. One week without her lips smashed against my mouth. One entire week without her sweet nectar sitting on my lips.

I had so much time to make up for.

Limbs tangled and lips firmly locked, we stumbled to the hallway. Making it to the bedroom wasn't going to happen, and that didn't matter to me. I would fuck her wherever we landed. When we reached the doorway, I leaned against the frame, whipping my shirt from my shoulders as she dropped to her knees.

Her skirt pooled around her feet as she tugged her blouse down, revealing her plump breasts and hardened nipples. I shucked my pants to the ground and revealed my stiff length that twitched eagerly at the feeling of her breath coating the tip. Her tongue extended next, a slow and sensuous motion that set my nerve-endings on fire.

Warm, wet strokes circled the tip of my cock as she cupped her breasts, propping them up and making them appear larger. She drooled over my shaft, soaking my length liberally with fluid as she swallowed my length with her breasts. The tip of my cock remained perched on her lips, saliva bubbling around the head and dripping down my shaft.

I groaned as I tangled my fingers into her hair, sweeping back her bangs to reveal her dark eyes that were committed to keeping me within her sight. Loud slurps erupted from her mouth as she suckled on the head of my cock. With her mouth sucking and her breasts stroking my shaft, I could have blown my load right there.

But I wanted more from her. I wanted to see what she would do. I wanted every inch of her to be pressed against me for as long as possible.

More drool trickled from her mouth, slicking my shaft as she bobbed up and down. Suction sounds echoed in the small hallway as I grunted with each slurp, eyelids fluttering whenever her warm mouth sank farther down my shaft. I gripped a chunk of her hair and held her steady as I stole her rhythm, thrusting into her hot, wet mouth.

Groans vibrated around my shaft. She held her breasts up for me to plunge between, arching her back to offer more of her to me. My senses soared when I noticed the way her lips bruised from her task, plump and pink with desire. Shivering, I yanked her mouth away from my cock and urged her to stand, stealing her lips as soon as she was upright.

My fingers sought her clit, the wet slit soaked to the brim with delicious nectar. I sank my tongue into her mouth as I vigorously rubbed her throbbing bud, sending shock waves through her body that appeared as violent shudders. Moans trailed from her lips to mine. I smiled through the kiss as I inserted two fingers into her channel.

More fluid gushed to greet my hand. I pinned her to the wall, pumping my fingers quickly into her channel as I released her lips and searched for her breasts. Perky nipples appeared within my field of vision, inviting me to lap and lick them sore. Squeaking moans escaped her bruised lips as I nudged my thumb against her clit, sliding the digit in tandem with my plunging fingers.

"Daddy..." she drawled with strained effort. "That feels *so* good..."

"Just wait until you feel my cock, baby girl."

She shuddered again, hands clutching my shoulders as I nursed on her right nipple. When she was close to the brink, I withdrew my fingers, watching with delight as she bucked her way toward me. She didn't want me to stop—but teasing her felt so *good*.

Whimpering incoherently wouldn't make me continue, and she knew that. I drew her to the bedroom, bending her over the dresser with the large mirror.

"Now you can see how I make you feel," I growled into her ear as I tore her skirt open to reveal her pert bottom. "And you can see how you make *me* feel."

"Yes, Daddy..."

Dedication sat in every syllable, her words a true testament to her commitment. She belonged to me. Every inch of her was mine, heart included, and no one would ever threaten to break us apart. I nudged her channel with the head of my cock as I wrapped my fingers around her throat, arching her back and forcing her to look into the mirror as I pierced her muff.

Surrender erupted on her features as her mouth widened into a perfect circular shape. I plunged into her depths, shivering as I felt her channel clench around my cock. I didn't rear back until I had claimed every bit of her insides, returning quickly to take more from her.

Rapid thrusts exploded from my hips, rocking the dresser against the wall and shaking the mirror. A ball of electricity coiled in my gut as I felt her tighten and relax in quick succession, channel trembling around my shaft and inspiring me to pick up my pace. Charged with desire, I focused on her face in the mirror, watching as pleasure and pain flashed across her features.

Within minutes, her body began to convulse. I

retained my rhythm, keeping it steady as she rode the wave of her orgasm. A great wail echoed in the bedroom as she came, inspiring me to follow shortly after her. Thrust after thrust blew that electric ball in my gut apart, sending lightning bolts through every one of my limbs.

I slammed into her bottom, buried myself to the hilt, and filled her with my seed, groaning with every spurt until I was spent. The moment I withdrew my cock was the moment I drew her onto the bed, wrapping her up in my arms to keep her close. Goosebumps decorated her skin wherever I kissed her and I kept up the movement, my cock hardening again as she wrapped her legs around me.

"I have something for you," I whispered weakly as I rested my head on the mattress.

"I thought you just gave it to me."

I chuckled. "It's in my pants."

She glanced at my cock and then focused on me. "I thought..."

"Go get Daddy's pants, baby girl."

No argument. Just response. And it was instantaneous, too.

I watched with pride as she retrieved my pants from the hallway, walking on wobbly legs. I laughed as she handed me my jeans and then sat crossed-legged on the mattress next to me.

I fished the ring from my pocket and held it between us. For a moment, her face didn't quite register her emotions. And then, she was crying, hard sobs that rocked her body toward me as she accepted the gold band.

"You're everything to me," I explained as I sat up and pressed my forehead to hers. She held my shoulders, clutching to me to steady herself. "You've always been everything to me. And now, I want to make that real."

"Daddy, I..."

"It's entirely up to you, okay?"

She sniffled, the crying subsiding as her eyes cleared of tears. She focused on me with a suddenly sober look in her eyes, the shock and lust having drifted into the background.

After a deep breath, she replied, "Yes."

"Really?"

"Yes, I'll marry you!"

I *whooped* loudly as I tackled her to the bed, nearly causing her to fumble the ring. As I slid it over her left-hand ring finger, I felt something burst in me. A cosmic explosion erupted in my chest, revealing a steel rope that connected the two of us together.

"Mates," she whispered while resting her heart over mine. "For life."

Chattering voices echoed from outside, interrupting our moment. I turned to focus my panther hearing the commotion, noticing how close the voices were to our yard. I glanced at Maria who shrugged, equally confused.

I urged her to clean up and get dressed, stealing kisses from her at every turn. We kissed our way to the foyer and then checked our reflection in the mirror before heading out to the porch. I glanced at the familiar truck sitting in front of April's home.

"A new shipment," Maria whispered. "Oh, that must be Sia!"

"Sia and Barry, huh?"

She nodded. "I ran into them about a week and a half ago. That's when I..."

Her voice caught in her throat as she stared at a tall man lingering near the alpha's porch with the rest of the group.

"Oh," she whispered. She turned to me then, taking my hands. "Landon?"

"Yes, baby girl?"

"I'm yours, okay? Nothing will ever change that."

I squinted. "What's happened? Are you okay?"

"That tall man over there," she explained slowly, "is my ex-boyfriend."

Flames sprouted in my soul, and my inner panther suddenly alerts me of everything that was happening around us. "Your ex?"

"Hopefully, he doesn't stick around."

"I sure hope not," I said while wrapping my arms possessively around her. "Because you belong to me. You're mine. Forever."

"Yes, Daddy," she whispered, heat laced in her words. "I belong to you *forever...*"

HELLO FRIENDS,

Thank you for reading another book about a sexy daddy doctor! I hope you enjoyed the fourth book in The Unbreakable Doctor series. Landon and Maria were truly meant for each other. They almost didn't survive with his dark secret, but they were redeemed in the end—because love brought them together.

What's going to happen when Josh, Maria's cocky ex-boyfriend, ends up falling for a woman so much younger than him? Will he remain the same jerk as always? Are his intentions true or will he try hard to make his past the present? If Sia could ever forgive his previous life, maybe they could be happy together...

Find out whether Josh can change his ways in the fifth book in the series by clicking HERE.

Happy reading! I look forward to seeing you again in another romance about a steaming hot doctor tiger daddy.

ALSO BY AMELIA WILSON